D1243418

DO LITTLE BABIES DREAM OF MU?

HUGENSLOP
PRESS

ISBN: 978-1-64786-188-9

The illustrations in this book were made with watercolors, pen, marker, crayon, and glitter paint on a variety of different types of paper. One of the meditating faces was made with marker on a whiteboard. The photograph of this face as well as the photograph on page 32 were taken by the author.

For my illustrators and in loving memory of my father
-S.B.

For my special mother
-H.B.

For Mama
-V.B.

"I really need you to put your soccer stuff on."

"Look."

"I like that, but your sister is acting a little sick and we've got a game to go to and we need to leave in less than 10 minutes and —"

4

"It's your Christmas List."

"Well, it's March, but thank you, honey."

She must be dreaming of her past life on the lost continent of Mu…

Mu

…and all she learned there.

In Mu, things are different.

For one, holidays are more frequent.

Some say that's due to the whims

of the Googly-Eyed Turtle who

lords over most of the celebrations.

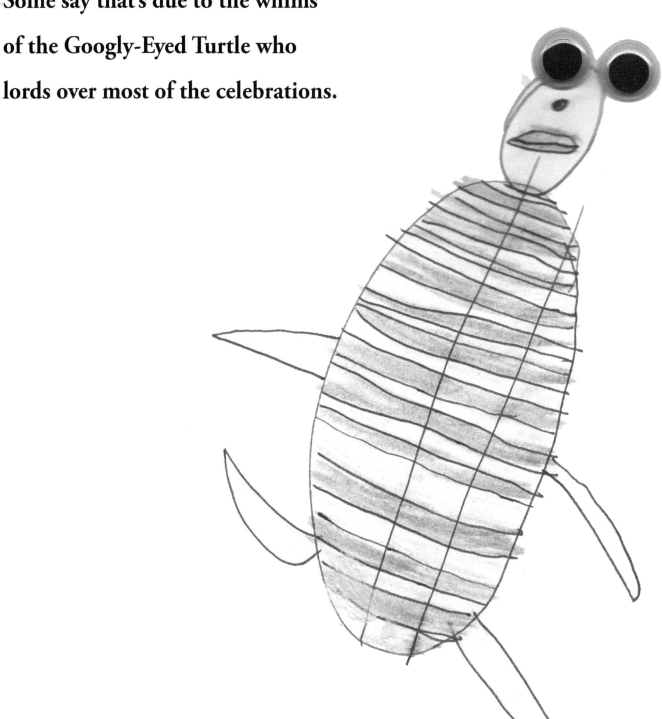

Most of the Children in Mu know that it's actually a result of an interdimensional wormhole

that causes Mu to complete an orbit of the Sun more frequently than the Earth.

Either way, the Children love to give gifts

as each holiday rolls around.

"Why do we put sprinkles in with the medicine?"

"That's a great question.

Honestly, I have no idea.

Can you grab your cleats please?"

School in Mu is taught in great fields of flowers.

Classes range from Sprinkle Storage...

to Squid Wrestling?

The curriculum is actually pretty wide open.

"I've been working on the railroad, all the live-long day! I've been working on the railroad, just to pass the time away."

"How do you all know that song?"

Most Children in Mu do a stint on the railroads.

The railroads there can be pretty colorful.

Some circle a rainbow-striped rabbit.

Others meander more freely.

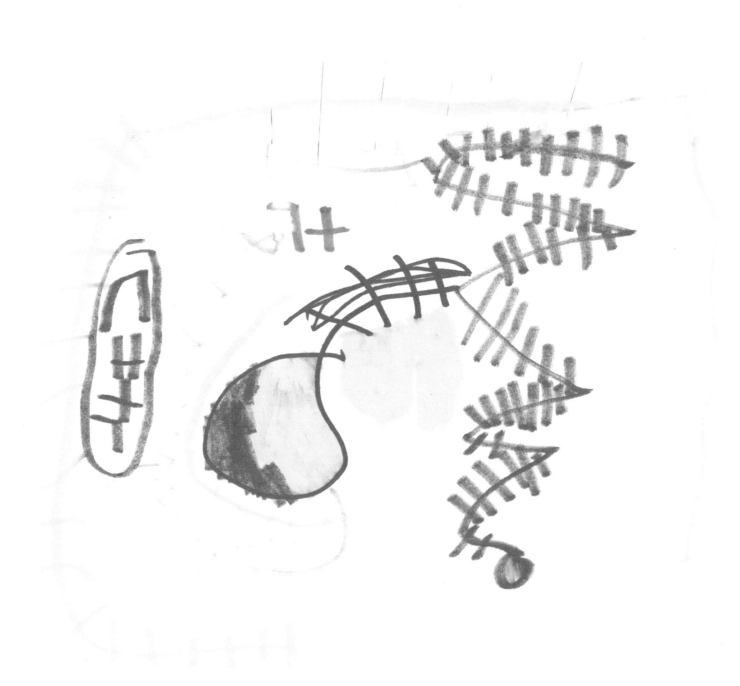

Still more simply do their own thing.

"So are you going to go into the game?"

"No."

"Do you want to go sit with your team at least?"

"No...I want to go home and eat Cheerios."

The Children in Mu do not defy authority for no reason.

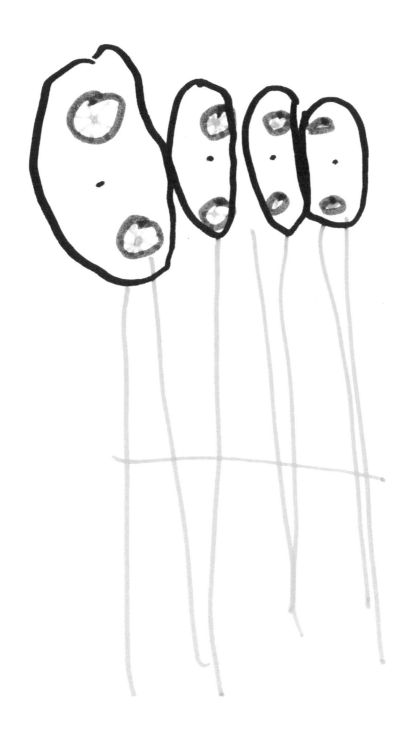

Instead, they question what is and why.

And, apparently...

...they do a lot of meditating.

"Daddy, bees!"

"Yeah."

"I'd like to sit and watch the bees for a little bit if that's OK."

"We can do that."

In Mu, the bees are a little bigger.

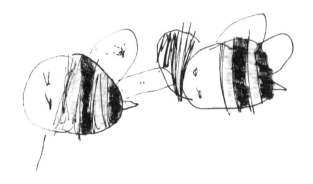

They usually come out at dusk to fly with the night parrots.

The Children have to act fast to get a good spot to watch, because, otherwise, the view can get a little obstructed.

"I miss Granddad. I wish he would come back."

"I didn't know you remembered."

The Children practice great feats of memory in Mu.

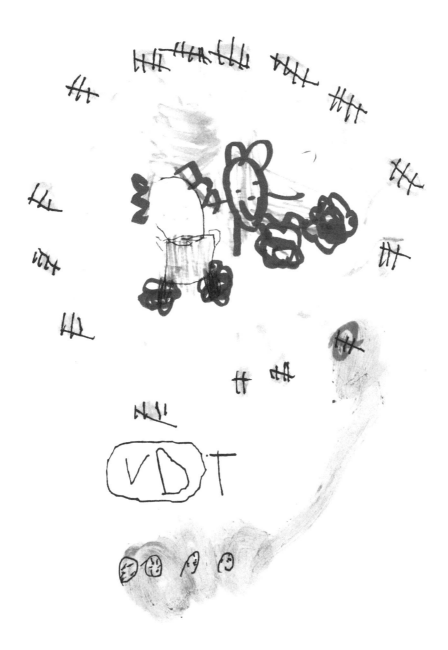

FUNES, they call it, the instant-recall pod.

It would be debilitating if used all the time, but the Children find periodic stints of total recall helpful for many things.

The pod-operator—you know, this guy—will lower a Child into the quicksand pit for a session.

"Where's Mommy?"

"She's on a work trip."

"When's she coming home?"

"Tomorrow."

"Sunset."

Mu has remarkable sunsets.

That's mostly on account of the blue and pink and green and brown tangs in the water off the coasts of Mu.

The tang is not a terribly noteworthy fish on its own.

But when the sun reflects off a family of them...

...they create something memorable.

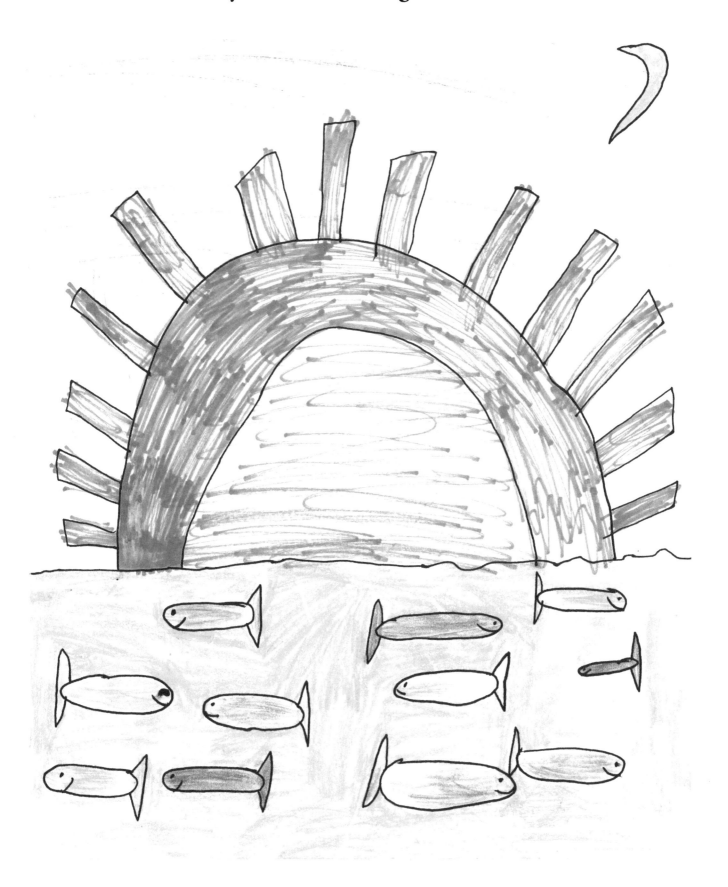

The End

About the Author and Illustrators

Stuart A. Burkhalter is the author of *Catawampus: The Fertility Process from a Man's Perspective* (2014), which, among other things, was named a Finalist in Foreword Reviews' INDIEFAB Book of the Year Awards: Autobiography & Memoir. Stuart is an attorney and lives in Nashville with his wife, Julie, and two daughters, Helen and Virginia.

Helen and Virginia Burkhalter are mostly full-time students right now. This is their first published work as illustrators.

CPSIA information can be obtained
at www.ICGtesting.com
Printed in the USA
LVHW071325200220
647628LV00004B/5